POKÉMON

HOW TO DRAW

JOHTO HEROES

D1371688

WRITTEN AND ILLUSTRATED BY RON ZALME

ISBN 978-0-545-24826-6

© 2010 Pokémon. © 1995-2010 Nintendo/Creatures Inc./GAME FREAK inc. ™ and ® and characters are trademarks of Nintendo. All rights reserved. Published by Scholastic Inc.
SCHOLASTIC and associated logos are trademarks and/or registered trademarks of Scholastic Inc.

12 11 10 9 8 7 6 5 4 3 2 1   10 11 12 13 14 15/0

Designed by Cheung Tai
Printed in the U.S.A.   40
First printing, August 2010

SCHOLASTIC INC.

| New York | Toronto | London | Auckland |
| Sydney | Mexico City | New Delhi | Hong Kong |

Pokémon Challenge: Get Ready to Draw!

Ever wanted to try drawing your favorite Pokémon? In the pages that follow, you'll get step-by-step instructions on sketching popular Pokémon like Chikorita, Cyndaquil, Totodile, and many more.

Before we start, you'll need some basic info! Read on, Trainer . . . and get ready to put your pencil to the test!

The Basic Tools

Here's what you'll need to get started . . .

- **Pencil** — Any basic graphite pencil can accomplish most drawing needs.
- **Paper** — Photocopy paper or tracing paper is terrific for sketching.
- **Eraser** — Try a soft one that won't smudge and has "edges" to get into tight spots.
- **Rulers, circle guides, ellipse (oval) guides, and shaped curves** — These help create a smooth, finished look for your drawing.
- **Color** — Try pens, markers, colored pencils, watercolors, paints, etc.

Practice Makes Perfect

This book contains fifteen interesting Pokémon broken down into a series of simple steps. You'll start each new drawing with a few simple, well-placed sketch lines to serve as a foundation upon which to build your drawing. These first lines, sketched in soft black pencil, are "action" lines, since they reveal the motion in each character's pose. Using the action lines as a guide, place some basic shapes, drawn here in blue, to create a framework. From there, you'll be able to add detail until each Pokémon is complete.

After all the sketching is done, clean up your drawing with your soft eraser, and then refine it! The idea is to get rid of the lines you used to build your drawing and concentrate on the linework that best identifies the character. To help you, the last step is a "clean" drawing with all the foundation lines removed so you can compare your sketch to the final pose.

Once you're happy with your drawing, it'll be up to you to decide how you'd most like to express yourself artistically! You can choose to ink your drawing, or trace it with marker . . . you can add color, texture, and even shading for that professional Pokémon look!

Getting in Shape

Circles, ovals, squares, rectangles, and triangles are the two-dimensional shapes you'll be working with when you put pencil to paper.

Spheres, cones, cubes, cylinders, and pyramids are the three-dimensional shapes that an artist must *think* in while drawing! Thinking in 3-D helps create an illusion of depth and volume in your artwork. It makes your final drawing look more convincing.

Ready, Get Set . . . Go!

Drawing takes practice, so don't get discouraged if you don't get the results you expect right away! Keep at it and your confidence in your abilities will grow.

Are you ready? Then grab a pencil and let's get started!

CHIKORITA

Chikorita loves to spend time in the sun. It uses the leaf on its head to get its own personal weather report. Chikorita's leaf smells sweet, but look out! It can be used for a dangerous Razor Leaf attack.

1 Look for the two black action lines — the long sweeping vertical one and the down-turned V shape of the horizontal one. Draw them carefully on your paper. Next, sketch the large blue circle and copy the crosshairs — these two crisscross lines will help you place Chikorita's features later. Finish with a line for the leaf and a forefoot.

2 Using what you drew in step 1 as a guide, line up the eyes and mouth on the crosshairs. Sketch the body shape carefully. Use the position of your action lines and basic shapes to judge proportion and position. Add the bottom line of the leaf on top of Chikorita's head.

POKÉMON STATS

TYPE: Grass

HEIGHT: 2' 11"

WEIGHT: 14.1 lbs.

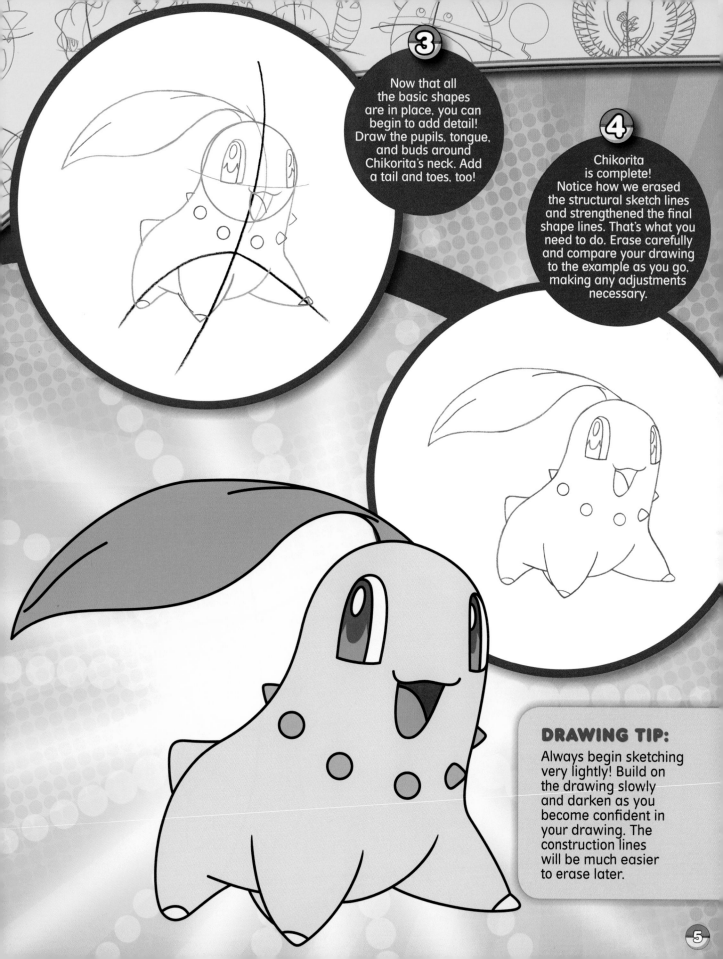

3 Now that all the basic shapes are in place, you can begin to add detail! Draw the pupils, tongue, and buds around Chikorita's neck. Add a tail and toes, too!

4 Chikorita is complete! Notice how we erased the structural sketch lines and strengthened the final shape lines. That's what you need to do. Erase carefully and compare your drawing to the example as you go, making any adjustments necessary.

DRAWING TIP:

Always begin sketching very lightly! Build on the drawing slowly and darken as you become confident in your drawing. The construction lines will be much easier to erase later.

CYNDAQUIL

Cyndaquil is a timid Pokémon who enjoys curling into a ball. But be warned: If Cyndaquil is startled, the flames on its back can turn into quite a blaze. Handle with care!

POKÉMON STATS

TYPE: Fire
HEIGHT: 1' 08"
WEIGHT: 17.4 lbs.

1 This time, the horizontal black action line sweeps upward. Copy both lines onto your paper. Next, sketch the head circle over the horizontal action line and the body circle below it. Note how the crosshairs establish the direction the face is pointing. Add a loose outline (on the right) to define a boundary for the flames . . . it doesn't need to be exact.

2 Add the nose and legs in position over your sketch. Next, place the mouth and eye, then put some flame detail along the back.

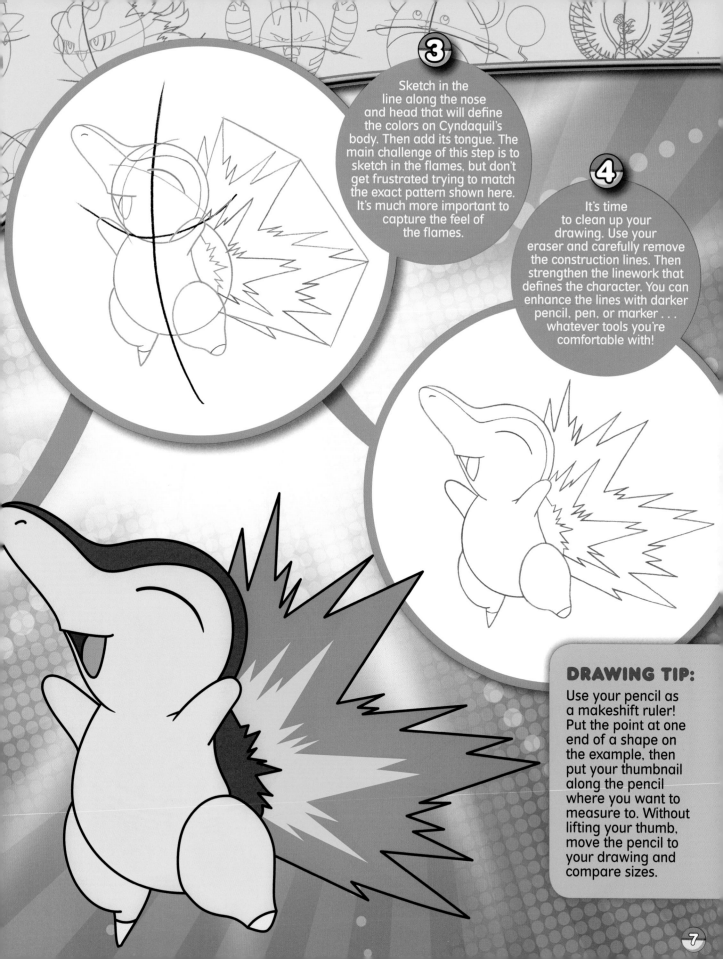

3

Sketch in the line along the nose and head that will define the colors on Cyndaquil's body. Then add its tongue. The main challenge of this step is to sketch in the flames, but don't get frustrated trying to match the exact pattern shown here. It's much more important to capture the feel of the flames.

4

It's time to clean up your drawing. Use your eraser and carefully remove the construction lines. Then strengthen the linework that defines the character. You can enhance the lines with darker pencil, pen, or marker . . . whatever tools you're comfortable with!

DRAWING TIP:

Use your pencil as a makeshift ruler! Put the point at one end of a shape on the example, then put your thumbnail along the pencil where you want to measure to. Without lifting your thumb, move the pencil to your drawing and compare sizes.

TOTODILE

A battler with super-strong jaws, Totodile will snap at just about anything that moves — even its own Trainer!

2

Sketch the eye shapes and then carefully add the nose and mouth. Now sketch in the arms and feet. You can also begin to add tail-spikes, starting with the one closest to the end of the tail.

1

Draw the action lines lightly and place the large head circle, with its crosshairs, on the vertical one. Next, locate and sketch the large oval for the hip of the leg. This will make it much easier to copy the shapes for the rest of the body and tail.

POKÉMON STATS

TYPE: Water
HEIGHT: 2' 00"
WEIGHT: 20.9 lbs.

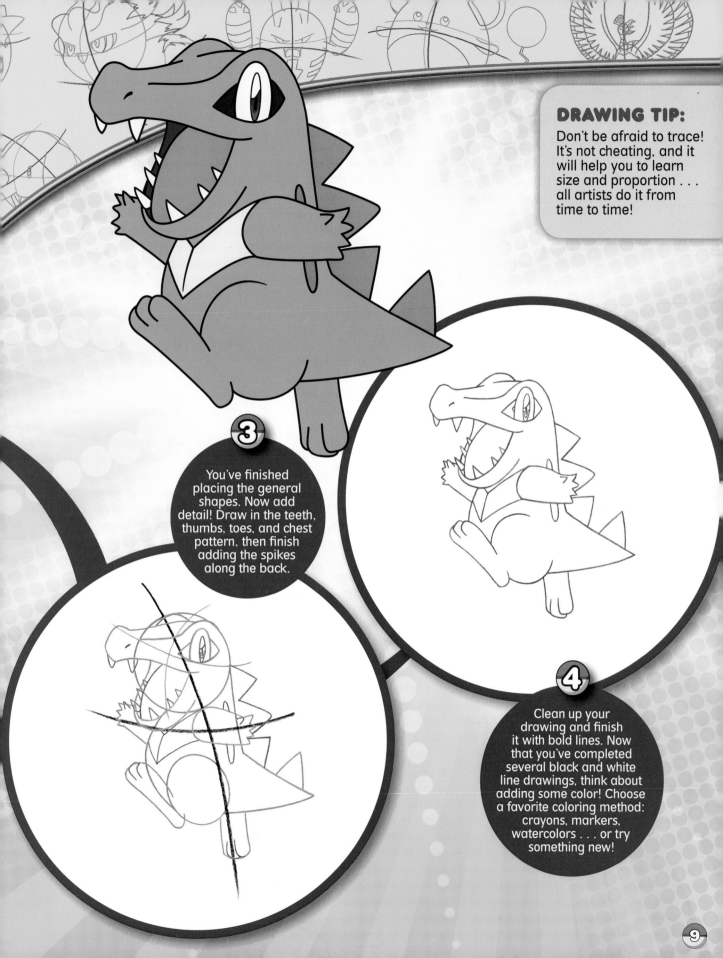

DRAWING TIP:
Don't be afraid to trace! It's not cheating, and it will help you to learn size and proportion . . . all artists do it from time to time!

3 You've finished placing the general shapes. Now add detail! Draw in the teeth, thumbs, toes, and chest pattern, then finish adding the spikes along the back.

4 Clean up your drawing and finish it with bold lines. Now that you've completed several black and white line drawings, think about adding some color! Choose a favorite coloring method: crayons, markers, watercolors . . . or try something new!

PHANPY

Though small in stature, Phanpy is surprisingly brawny. It can easily pick up and carry an adult human. It can also be affectionate and nudge people with its snout. But beware: Phanpy doesn't know its own strength, and it might send you zooming through the air!

1

Begin with the two black action lines and then sketch the very large circle for Phanpy's head. Add the crosshairs that determine the way it's facing. Now sketch the large body shape and proceed to step two!

②

Using the head-circle as a guide, sketch in the large ear and snout. Check your proportions! With a few straight lines and some simple curves, you can define the shape and positioning of the feet.

DRAWING TIP:

You don't have to use black pencil for all your drawings. Try sketching lightly in a color, like blue, for structure, and then strengthen your lines with black or another intense color.

POKÉMON STATS

TYPE: Ground
HEIGHT: 1' 08"
WEIGHT: 73.9 lbs.

③

Detail time! Finish the eye and mouth, add detail to the snout and ear, and sketch in the toes. Did you remember the rear foot?

④

Finish your drawing by cleaning up with your eraser and strengthening your outlines. Then have some fun with color! Interested in a challenge? Try drawing Phanpy facing to the right!

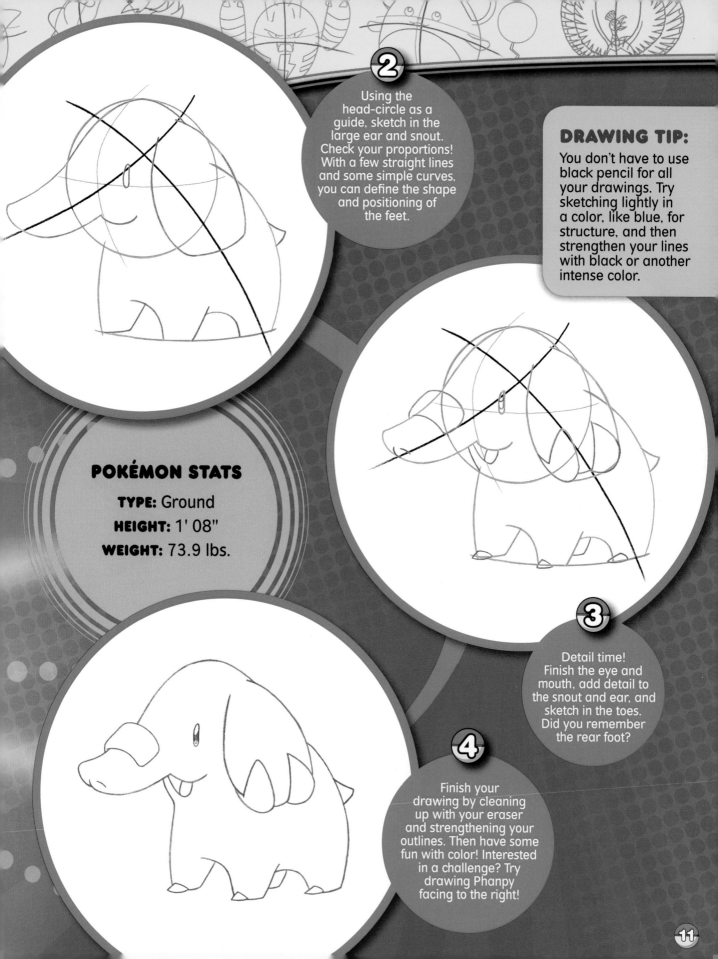

MARILL

Marill uses its tail as a float to help it dive underwater, where it feeds on plants at the bottom of rivers. The ball on the end of its tail is filled not with air, but with a special oil that's lighter than water.

POKÉMON STATS

TYPE: Water
HEIGHT: 1' 04"
WEIGHT: 18.7 lbs.

1

Begin with the usual curved, crossed action lines and place the very large oval over them. Notice that it's almost a circle, but just a bit pinched toward the top. Add the crosshairs for the features on Marill's face, then draw a smaller circle to the right of the big one.

2

Sketch the eyes, nose, and mouth along the crosshair axis, and then add the two large ovals for ears. Finish roughing in your character by adding the arms and feet.

3 The rest is detail! Draw the inner ear ovals, and then make a large circle on Marill's chest area to define its color design. Connect the smaller tail circle to the main body with two jagged lines. It's not important that they be drawn exactly as long as they get across the right idea.

4 Clean up with your eraser, and focus on the shapes and details. Compare your drawing to the example. Have you missed anything? Make any corrections necessary and consider your color options!

DRAWING TIP:

It's not necessary to buy circle guides and other shapes. You can use various household items like buttons, coins, cups, and cans . . . anything round can work as a guide!

MISDREAVUS

This spooky prankster enjoys sneaking up behind people to startle them or yank their hair! Misdreavus feeds on the fear that its shrieks create in its targets.

2

Use the crosshairs as guides to locate and draw the eyes and mouth. When they're done, their position will help you figure out where to place the flowing lines at the back of Misdreavus's head. Add a ring of circles like a necklace around the neck . . . use the action lines like a guide!

1

The action lines are very similar to those for Marill, but the horizontal line is much lower. See how such a slight change at the beginning of a sketch can affect the way it turns out? Make the very large circle for the head, and then add the skirt-like shape to the bottom.

POKÉMON STATS

TYPE: Ghost

HEIGHT: 2' 04"

WEIGHT: 2.2 lbs.

3

Add the rest of the pupil detail to define the eyes. Then finish the head and make it more wispy-looking. Focus on the overall look, not how many little curves or points there are.

4

Grab your eraser and do your usual clean-up routine! Artists are known for their creativity, so try something new to make your drawing special. Perhaps a different coloring technique or different sketching materials?

DRAWING TIP:

If you've gotten comfortable always drawing with your left or right hand, try switching hands to see what you can achieve!

CROBAT

Crobat are nocturnal creatures — that is, they are active mostly at night. Their double sets of wings allow them to fly quickly and silently, making them very difficult to detect!

POKÉMON STATS

TYPE: Poison-Flying
HEIGHT: 5' 11"
WEIGHT: 165.3 lbs.

1 Draw your action lines (note the Y shape of the horizontal line!) and then, where they cross, draw the shield-like body shape. Add two more wing lines curving off the horizontal action line.

2 Along the axis of your crosshairs, line up the features . . . and make sure to use fierce eyes! Draw the long ovals for ears, and then add structure to the wing shapes.

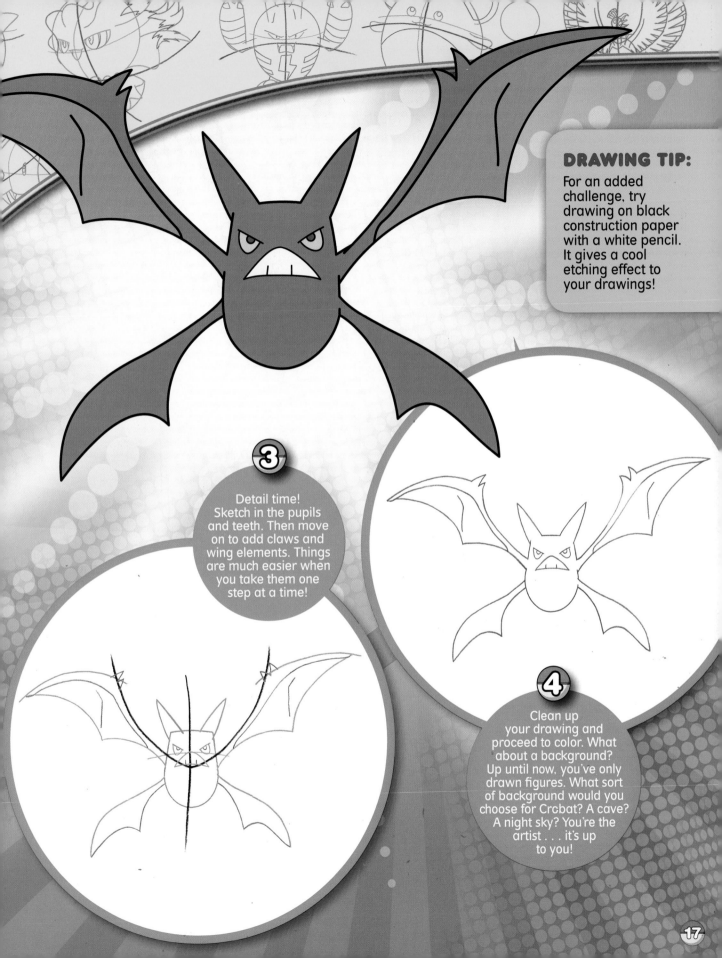

3

Detail time! Sketch in the pupils and teeth. Then move on to add claws and wing elements. Things are much easier when you take them one step at a time!

4

Clean up your drawing and proceed to color. What about a background? Up until now, you've only drawn figures. What sort of background would you choose for Crobat? A cave? A night sky? You're the artist . . . it's up to you!

TEDDIURSA

When the crescent-shaped mark on Teddiursa's forehead begins to glow, that means it's found honey! The Little Bear Pokémon licks its paws frequently, since they are always soaked in honey.

2
Draw the eyes, nose, and mouth in position over the guides, then sketch in the arms, feet, and tail. Last, but not least, put in some detail for the ears.

1
Action lines, large head circle, crosshairs, body shape, and ears. No matter how complex the drawing, you break it down into a series of easier steps: foundation, basic shapes, and detail.

POKÉMON STATS

TYPE: Normal
HEIGHT: 2' 00"
WEIGHT: 19.4 lbs.

4

Erase your unwanted sketch lines, and then strengthen the lines you want to keep. Now that you know the basics, try drawing Teddiursa in a pose of your own! The shapes will remain basically the same, but the positioning will change.

3

Add that crescent on Teddiursa's fore-head! And don't forget the cheek lines, claws, tongue, and toes. Almost done!

TYROGUE

Tyrogue are tough for their size. Hotheaded and short-tempered, they slug first and ask questions later. That means that they're often nursing injuries, but their boundless energy keeps them on the attack anyway . . . even against larger foes!

1 In a smooth flowing motion, sketch in the two action lines. The more fluid they appear, the more life your drawing will have. As usual, position the basic shapes . . . head circle, hands, hips.

DRAWING TIP:

Try drawing your first draft on tracing paper. If you use a layer for each step, you won't have to erase as much.

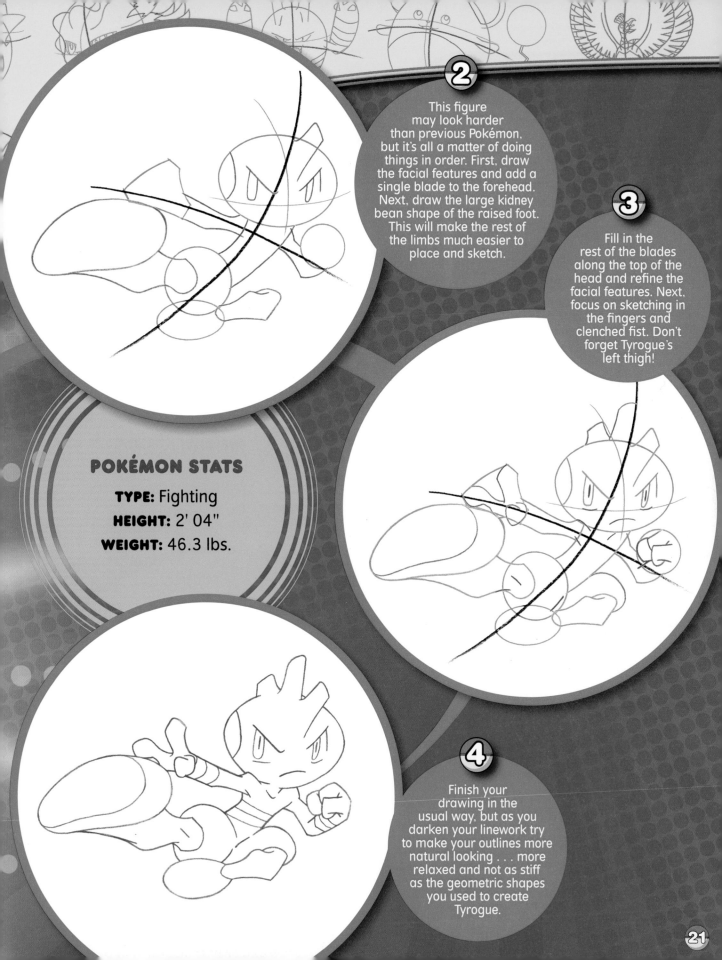

2

This figure may look harder than previous Pokémon, but it's all a matter of doing things in order. First, draw the facial features and add a single blade to the forehead. Next, draw the large kidney bean shape of the raised foot. This will make the rest of the limbs much easier to place and sketch.

3

Fill in the rest of the blades along the top of the head and refine the facial features. Next, focus on sketching in the fingers and clenched fist. Don't forget Tyrogue's left thigh!

POKÉMON STATS

TYPE: Fighting
HEIGHT: 2' 04"
WEIGHT: 46.3 lbs.

4

Finish your drawing in the usual way, but as you darken your linework try to make your outlines more natural looking . . . more relaxed and not as stiff as the geometric shapes you used to create Tyrogue.

ELEKID

Elekid creates its own electricity by spinning its arms, causing its horns to flicker. Unfortunately, it can't save up the energy it makes. But that doesn't stop it from playing happily in severe thunderstorms!

POKÉMON STATS

TYPE: Electric
HEIGHT: 2' 00"
WEIGHT: 51.8 lbs.

1 After sketching the two action lines, locate and place the large body oval . . . and double-check your proportions! Add the two arms to the sides of the body shape.

2 Line up the facial features to the crosshair and horizontal action lines. Pencil in the two large horns on top of Elekid's head. Use two ovals for the feet, then add claws to the hands.

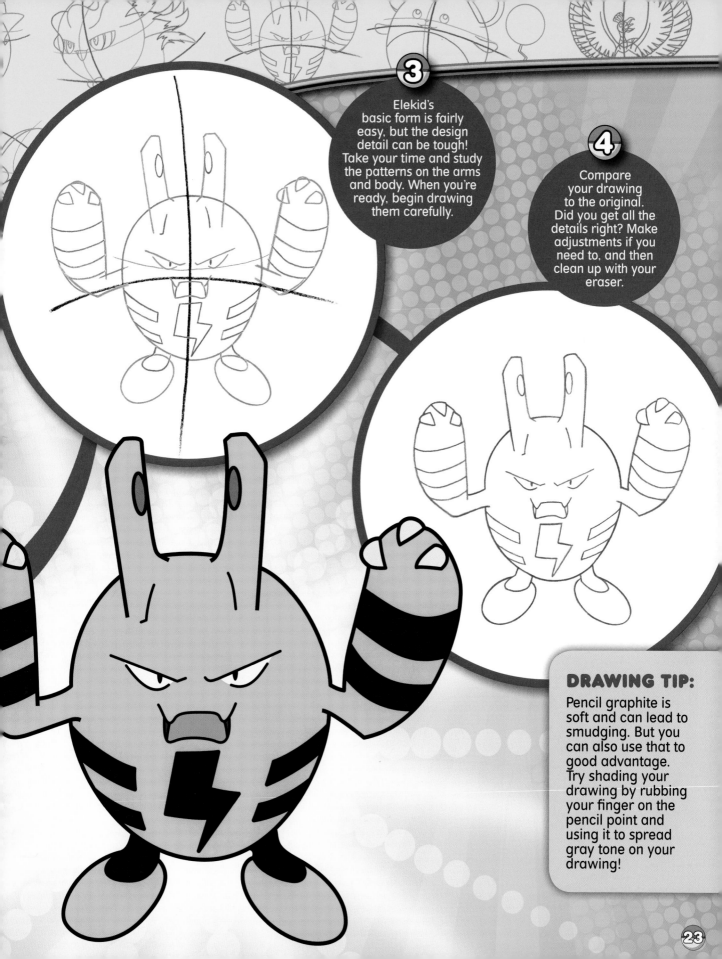

3

Elekid's basic form is fairly easy, but the design detail can be tough! Take your time and study the patterns on the arms and body. When you're ready, begin drawing them carefully.

4

Compare your drawing to the original. Did you get all the details right? Make adjustments if you need to, and then clean up with your eraser.

DRAWING TIP:

Pencil graphite is soft and can lead to smudging. But you can also use that to good advantage. Try shading your drawing by rubbing your finger on the pencil point and using it to spread gray tone on your drawing!

GIRAFARIG

Girafarig actually has *two* brains, one in its head and one in its tail! This allows the Long Neck Pokémon to protect its hindquarters from sneak attacks by biting with its tail.

2

Add eyes and facial detail to both the head and tail . . . and place a horn on top of the head as well. Study and carefully copy the front and back legs. Take your time and look for the basic shapes in the leg forms.

1

Start your sketch by lightly drawing the two action lines. Once you're done, add the circle for Girafarig's shoulder, then draw the head circle above it and connect the two to form a neck. Finally, draw the oval for that biting tail!

POKÉMON STATS

TYPE: Normal-Psychic

HEIGHT: 4' 11"

WEIGHT: 91.5 lbs.

24

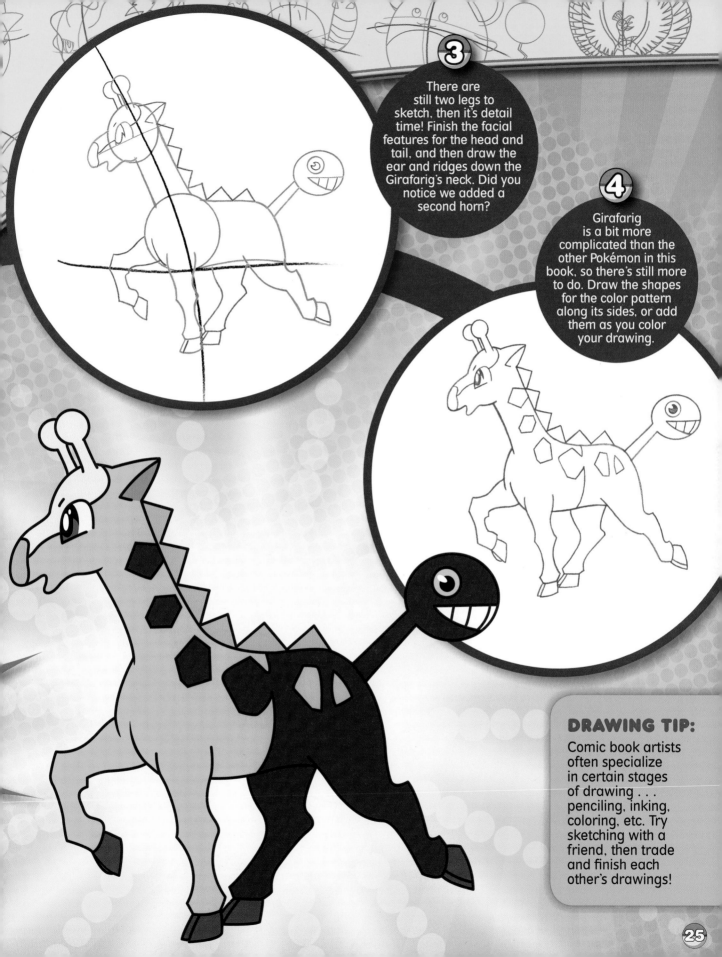

3

There are still two legs to sketch, then it's detail time! Finish the facial features for the head and tail, and then draw the ear and ridges down the Girafarig's neck. Did you notice we added a second horn?

4

Girafarig is a bit more complicated than the other Pokémon in this book, so there's still more to do. Draw the shapes for the color pattern along its sides, or add them as you color your drawing.

DRAWING TIP:

Comic book artists often specialize in certain stages of drawing . . . penciling, inking, coloring, etc. Try sketching with a friend, then trade and finish each other's drawings!

CELEBI

Sometimes known as the "guardian of the forest," Legendary Pokémon Celebi has the power to travel through time . . . though it usually appears only in times of peace.

POKÉMON STATS

TYPE: Psychic-Grass
HEIGHT: 2' 00"
WEIGHT: 11 lbs.

1 As you begin your sketch, study the action lines. Make the large oval for the head and place a smaller one below it for the body. Further down, you'll need an even smaller oval for Celebi's foot.

2 The crosshairs are mostly used to place the eyes and mouth, but you can also use the horizontal one to help locate the end-point for the head. Sketch in the arm shapes and finish the forms for the legs. Almost there!

4 That's about it! Do the usual cleanup and you've got another Pokémon to add to your Pokédex! (Note: The colors on Celebi are soft blends . . . a perfect opportunity to try paint or watercolor!)

3 Using the forms you've already sketched, begin to add the detail that defines Celebi . . . antennae, wings, etc. Pay close attention to how the eyes are drawn and how the crosshairs guide the direction the character is facing.

HO-OH

Ho-Oh's feathers can gleam in seven different colors. This Legendary Pokémon leaves a colorful rainbow behind it as it soars endlessly through the sky. Seeing a Ho-Oh is said to bring eternal happiness, so be on the lookout!

2

Sketch in the beak, neck, and feet first, and then add the boxy shape to the top of the head to contain the head feathers. Now use the big round circles from the first step to place the feathers. It's not important to copy every single feather exactly as long as you get the effect right.

1

Ho-Oh is probably the most challenging Pokémon to draw in this book, but it's all a matter of simplifying. All those feathers look intimidating, but they're really just the same shape repeated many times. Start with the action lines, then move on to the basic shapes.

POKÉMON STATS

TYPE: Fire-Flying
HEIGHT: 12' 06"
WEIGHT: 438.7 lbs.

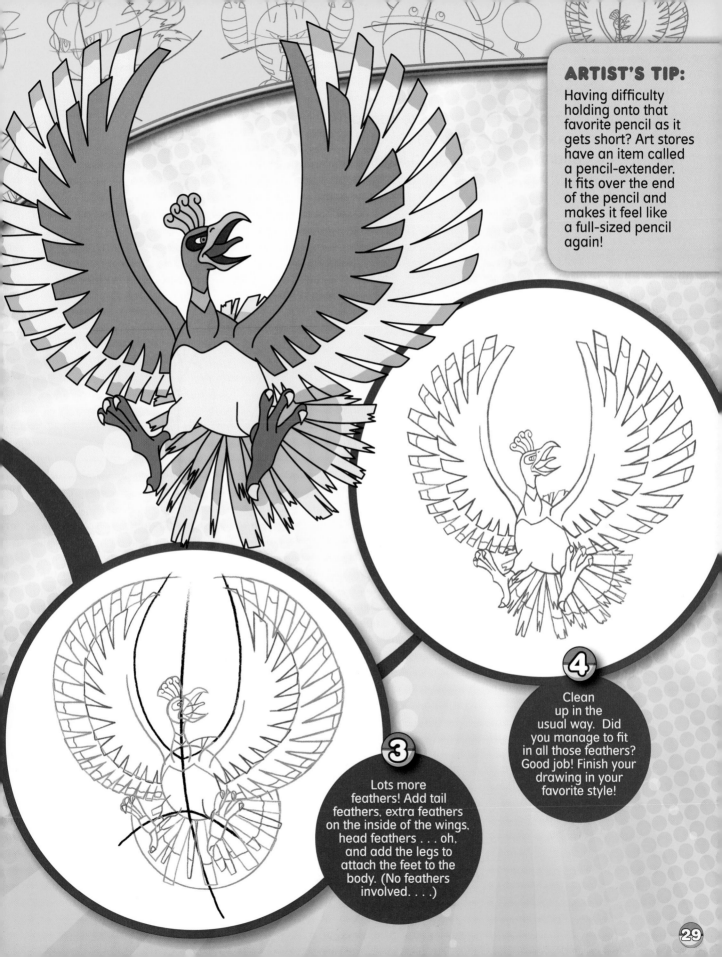

Having difficulty holding onto that favorite pencil as it gets short? Art stores have an item called a pencil-extender. It fits over the end of the pencil and makes it feel like a full-sized pencil again!

4

Clean up in the usual way. Did you manage to fit in all those feathers? Good job! Finish your drawing in your favorite style!

3

Lots more feathers! Add tail feathers, extra feathers on the inside of the wings, head feathers . . . oh, and add the legs to attach the feet to the body. (No feathers involved. . . .)

LUGIA

Legendary Pokémon Lugia prefers to spend its time sleeping in deep-sea trenches . . . and that might be a good thing! According to legend, if Lugia flaps its wings, the power unleashed can cause a forty-day storm!

1

This time three action lines are needed: The vertical one sets the pose for the figure, and the two upward sweeping lines form the wings. Once they're sketched, draw the body oval, the tail shape, and the head. Then move on to step two!

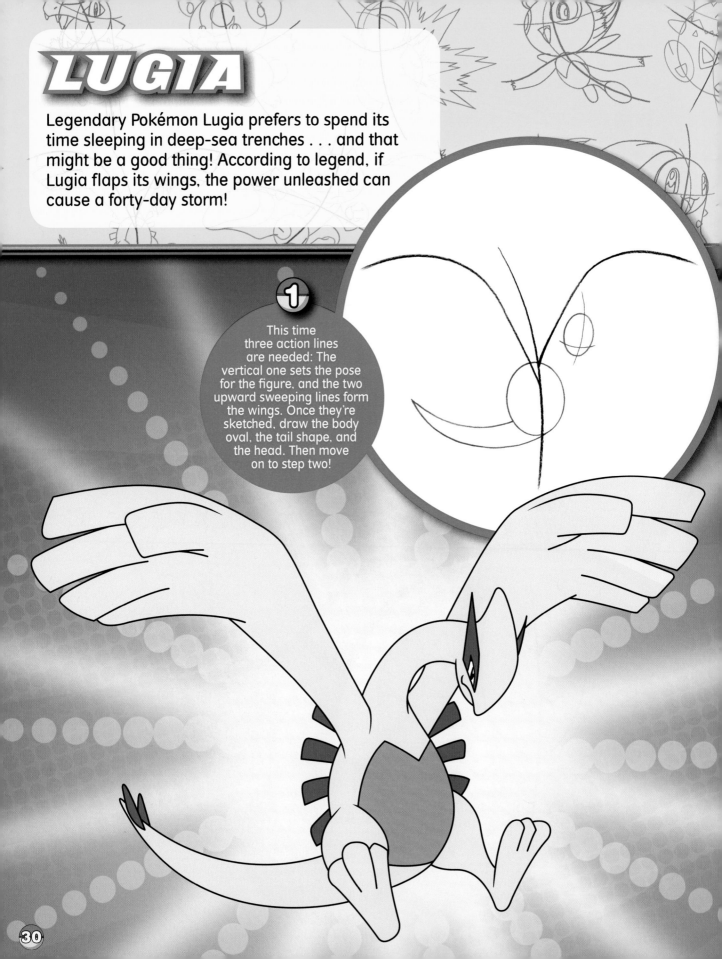

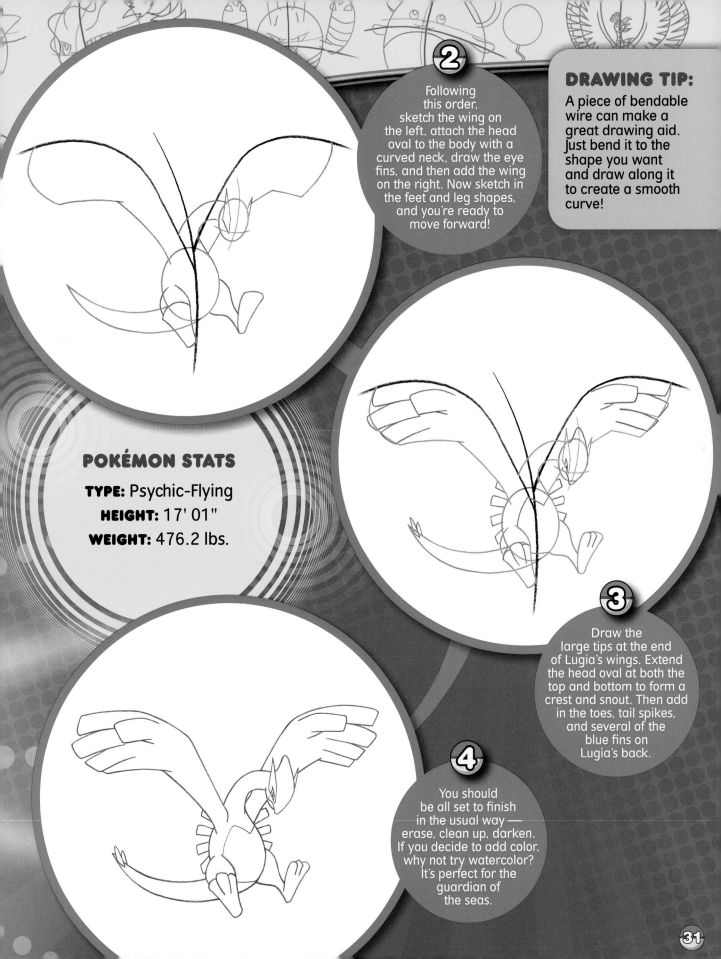

②

Following this order, sketch the wing on the left, attach the head oval to the body with a curved neck, draw the eye fins, and then add the wing on the right. Now sketch in the feet and leg shapes, and you're ready to move forward!

DRAWING TIP:

A piece of bendable wire can make a great drawing aid. Just bend it to the shape you want and draw along it to create a smooth curve!

POKÉMON STATS

TYPE: Psychic-Flying
HEIGHT: 17' 01"
WEIGHT: 476.2 lbs.

③

Draw the large tips at the end of Lugia's wings. Extend the head oval at both the top and bottom to form a crest and snout. Then add in the toes, tail spikes, and several of the blue fins on Lugia's back.

④

You should be all set to finish in the usual way — erase, clean up, darken. If you decide to add color, why not try watercolor? It's perfect for the guardian of the seas.

TOGEPI

Let's end our drawing adventure on a happy note — with Togepi. The Spike Ball Pokémon's shell is filled with joy . . . and it will share its happiness with anyone who can awaken it and make it stand up!

1 After copying the simple set of crisscross action lines, draw the very large circle shape for the body. Sketch the two crosshairs and add the simple ovals for the feet.

DRAWING TIP:
The steps you've learned are not just for Pokémon . . . apply them to all your drawings. How would *you* be constructed step-by-step?

2 Add three of the spikes on top of Togepi's head, then draw its face. The jagged lines of its shell don't need to be perfect as long as the right feel is there. Make sure they follow a curve around the shell, so your drawing will have some dimension to it.

4 Get rid of those construction lines and finish up in your favorite style! Remember, you're the artist, so decisions about how to create are yours to make. Imagination and experimentation are the best tools at your disposal, so use them!

3 If you didn't add the arms and toes in the last step, add them now! Then sketch in two more spikes on top of the head. Finish this step by drawing the triangular design shapes on its shell.

POKÉMON STATS

TYPE: Normal
HEIGHT: 1' 00"
WEIGHT: 3.3 lbs.

Well done! **Our journey with these popular Pokémon is ending, but your journey as a Pokémon artist is just beginning. Now you have the tools and knowledge to "capture" any and all Pokémon you encounter on paper! Collect them all, fill a book, and have fun!**